Sweetheart in the dark

I0625588

© 2017 Urquhart Randolph

Published by Glofton llc

Table Of Contents

Subscribe
visit us
Enroll in our VIP list.
Be the first to be notified on our latest published
book.
Downloading for free gifts.

Disclaimer

This is a work of fiction. Names, characters, organizations, spots, occasions and occurrences are either the results of the creator's creative energy or utilized as a part of an invented way. Any similarity to real people, living or dead, or genuine occasions is absolutely adventitious.

ISBN:9781946792280

Published by Glofton llc

CHAPTER 1

Living in National City, California, Annie had spent two lonely years after James – her husband – passed away. Though his corpse was never found, he was alleged to have died in a fatal air strike attack on Naval Base Point Loma by some unknown militant group. Before then, Annie was a happy comfortable housewife with two kids, Jane and Peter, who were eight and eleven years old respectively. James was a Master Chief Officer in the U.S.A Navy and the salary was better than good.

After his death, James' insurance relief, bank account balance and other Government compensations were not good enough to keep up with an already existing $700 monthly mortgage payment, combined with the tuition and upkeep expenses of her minors.

In just two years after James' alleged death, she alternated between seven different jobs in a bid to find a sustainable income but the salary wasn't good enough – her highest level of education was high school. After two years, she found a sustainable solution in online work-at-home jobs.

Everything was working just fine till on one Saturday afternoon, she stumbled upon the key to James' old forsaken safe. It was sitting somewhere behind the TV. She had no special interest in that particular safe because she knew James used to put irrelevant stuff in there – mainly old school test results.

Nevertheless, she opened up the safe and found no valuables other than a bunch of scrappy papers and an old video camera. She put some batteries in, turned it on and viewed the content which included sweet memories of their family life like Peter's first birthday party, Jane's one-day-old baby pictures and videos, their vacation trip to New Orleans etc.

She watched them in high spirits, feeling elated and would have relished traveling into the past to relive those moments. She spent about two hours watching the videos with Jane and Peter, and they loved it. It brought back fond memories of their dad and they just never wanted to end it. But little did Annie know that she was about unearthing the most startling revelation of her life. She lurched upon one never-seen video recording of James.

She took particular interest to this video since the date suggested it was the last recorded video on James' video camera, not long before the date of his demise.

As she tapped the play button, her cheeks burst into a broad smile, triggered by the sight of James' lovely looks – his bright brown pupil, smooth skin and curly black hair. In the video recording, James was seated in a chair but had a saddened look on his face. He began to speak, 'Hi Annie, this message is exclusively yours; highly confidential, and I require that no other hears this.'

As if moved by an electromagnetic force, she tapped the pause button spontaneously with her right forefinger. She wondered what could have been so confidential that James had never told her while alive. She grew extremely anxious and wondered what the content might be.

Annie smiled at the kids and said, 'This is a private message from your dad to me. Go have your lunch while I take some time off to listen.' They were worried and reluctant –wanting to watch too – but she would not take their word against hers.

Annie walked into her room, locked the door behind her and shut the windows, as if barricading her room against violent strangers. She tapped the play button and the video continued:

'Annie, 'I would have to fake my death. I know it's wrong but it's the only way to keep you and the kids alive. By the time you see this video, I'm sure I would have been presumed dead. I need not have made this recording but I just don't want you to bear so much unnecessary pain. I just want you to cheer up and make the kids happy. Please delete this video as soon as possible, before someone else sees it. It's much complicated than you think. I'm sorry dear, but I'll get things sorted out so we can reunite again. I love you dear. Please, discard this recording!!!'

She was completely shocked and saddened, yet felt a little joyful in hope. She burst into tears and sobbed quietly, not wanting her kids to hear. The revelation that James wasn't dead put some gladness in her heart. However, the fact that she had no idea where he was, in what condition he lived and when she was going to see him again was so depressing to her.

For some reasons apparent to her, she did not discard the recording. Not that she forgot, but she had some strings of emotions attached to it and wanted to watch it over and over again. Meanwhile, all that while, Peter had been eavesdropping from the corner of Annie's window. Though he couldn't grasp the exact words and information in the video, he knew whatever was in there made her mom cry and he was more than curious to find out.

Not long afterwards, Jane came knocking at her door. Annie hastily reshuffled some stuffs in her wardrobe and hid the camera beneath them before letting her in. Peter got a visual of her every action and so Annie's hiding compartment was no secret to Peter. He got down, walked back into the house, and figured out what to do.

CHAPTER 2

Annie had not been her usual self since finding the video a week ago. She spent sleepless nights, figuring out what to do; where to start from; whom to contact; where to go. Thoughts and ideas never ceased to flood her mind. However, she knew that whatever it was that could make an American-trained marine officer flee for his and his family's life must have been something really scary.

Meanwhile, Peter had been making frantic attempts to get to the camera throughout the week but Annie's work-at-home job meant she was often in the house and Peter hadn't gotten that loose opportunity yet. Jane wasn't making things any easier for her mom either as she kept pestering her with questions about what her dad had said in the video.

Apparently, Annie had told her James said he loved them and that they are all he'd ever had. Jane, however, didn't understand why she wasn't allowed to see the video but she chose to believe what her mom told her. On the other hand, Peter was not falling for such cheap lies and was really pissed.

Annie wanted to tell them the truth but she herself was absolutely confused; didn't understand what was at stake and she knew it was a highly classified information which would be perilous if not handled cautiously. Despite her frantic efforts to convince him, curious little Peter did not give up on his quest and he found a way to outsmart her.

Peter knew he couldn't trust Jane on this matter because Jane tells almost everything to her mom. He wasn't gonna take that chance but per his masterplan, he needed Jane.

After breakfast that Saturday morning, he approached Jane at the kitchen and incensed her to attend the community's kids' fun games. Unlike Peter, Jane loved the community games so much but since her dad died and her mother got super busy with job schedules, Jane hadn't got any taste of it in the last two years. But now with a much more flexible work schedule, Jane knew her mom had more time on her hands at home.

She ran to her mom excitedly and demanded that she took her to the games, reminding her that her dad would have if he was still alive. Annie was absolutely surprised and wondered how she had remembered those games all of a sudden but having just gone through a hell of a week, Annie didn't want to add a disappointment to Jane's already existing worries.

At 10:00am, Annie set off with Jane to the Community's Children's Park, leaving James alone at home and that was exactly what he had planned in mind. Peter ran to Annie's bedroom and turned the knob but surprisingly, it was locked. It was unusual of her to lock it. He sighed, was frustrated and yet more certain than ever that his mom was hiding the true content. By 11am, he had tried breaking through the door with various tools – from the kitchen and the garage – but all his efforts proved futile. However, he knew he wasn't gonna get such an opportunity again.

He figured out another plan – the window. He walked out to Annie's window and hurled a spanner into it. The glasses in the window crashed completely but he wasn't tall enough to climb in. Yet, the hyperactive Peter didn't give up.

He walked into the house to fetch a dining chair which he used as a platform of elevation to get himself through the window but he got the kind of entry that anyone wouldn't want to experience. He tumbled onto the floor, fell into the broken pieces of glass and cut himself badly.

Paying very little attention to the injuries, he lifted himself off the floor and moved straight towards his mom's wardrobe, sneaked his blood stained hands through her clothing and reached for the camera which was wrapped up and kept in a gift box. He was so bent on finding out its contents that he worried little about the severe injuries he had sustained. *I would rather find out and die than stay alive and be deprived of this information*, he thought. His right thigh took a very deep cut and was oozing out volumes of blood. After finally watching the video, he wished to get up but he had lost a lot of blood and was too weak. He lied helplessly on the floor, groaning in anguish.

At 12:30pm, Annie and Jane were returning along with Mark – James' best friend and also a Naval Officer. Mark had been visiting them twice every month since James' death. Just about fifty meters away from their home, Annie noticed her window was burglarized and her dining chair was standing beneath it.

She freaked out, almost bumping the car into a passerby. Millions of horrifying thoughts sprang into her brains and she got extremely scared. Everyone in the car figured it was a burglary assault. She was gripped with fear; not knowing the fate of Peter and not sure what the outcome would be if she went in.

She was torn between two actions – whether to drive Jane to a safe place and return for Peter or risk both of their lives for Peter's – but Mark calmed her down, assuring her he would take charge of the situation. He got down and asked her to drive about fifty meters away and wait for an all-clear signal.

Mark approached the house in a professional military manner. He peeped through the window and saw Peter lying down in a pool of blood. He rushed to inspect other parts of the house to ensure it was safe and finding it was, he signaled Annie to drive over. She ran into the house and nervously opened the door at his order, constantly asking Mark, 'Where is Peter? Where is Peter?' As the door opened, they saw Peter lying down unconscious and severely injured.

They wondered what had happened. Even though the camera was laying on the floor beside Peter, it rang no bell in Annie's mind at that moment. While Annie sunk to the ground in tears, thinking Peter had been murdered, Mark carried him precariously off the floor and rushed him out. He yelled at Annie to follow him, saying Peter wasn't dead. She sprang to her feet, raced after Mark into the car and sped off to the nearest hospital.

CHAPTER 3

Upon their arrival, the emergency department took over. Mark quickly drove home with Jane so she could freshen up while he cleaned up the mess in the house but Annie stayed at the hospital. Some minutes later, the doctors confirmed that Peter wasn't dead but was in a mild coma due to excessive loss of blood. Annie was glad he was still alive but was frustrated that the doctors had no idea when he would regain consciousness.

Arriving home, Jane freshened up while Mark fixed the mess in Annie's room. He took the video camera and scrolled through the videos. All along, Mark was privy to James' intentions to fake his death but he was absolutely surprised to find out he had foolishly recorded such a video despite the risk at stake.

It wasn't long before he could hear police sirens approaching from a distance. He quickly deleted the video and hid the camera elsewhere in the house.

The police detectives inspected the place, took them through some rounds of questionings and investigations before driving off with them to the hospital. They reached the hospital around 4pm. Anna, though devastated, forced a cheerful smile as she saw Jane and Mark approaching. Right after she was done hugging Mark and Jane, the detectives took her in for some interrogations which lasted about ten minutes. They couldn't make any conclusive judgments as yet.

The only logical assumptions they could make were that; Peter had injured himself in an attempt to steal or take something very valuable from the room or else; there was another person(s) that needed something very valuable from the room and used him as a camouflage to cover their tracks. Whichever be the case, the best answers lied with the kid himself.

Annie sat quietly by Mark who had Jane's head on his laps. As he patted Jane softly, he began to reflect on some memories: Mark got married six months before James and Annie did but got divorced two years later.

He'd never tried any relationship since but two weeks ago, when he visited and was in Annie's room, Annie expressed her admiration for him, her sexual attraction towards him and her longing desire to have him. Before he could utter a word, she lurched unto his lips with a passionate kiss which led to an unexpected round of sex. Mark was completely disgusted after everything and felt like a betrayer. Early the next morning, before Annie woke up, he left.

Annie, ignorant at the time, was certain her husband was dead but Mark wasn't sure if he was, although he never mentioned it to any. He wasn't sure where in the world he could be either. Annie was a lovely lady to behold and had always been the woman of Mark's dreams but obviously, she was the very one he felt he could never have.

They sat speechlessly by each other in Peter's ward for about ten minutes before Mark got up, laid Jane in the visitors' couch, and requested to speak privately with Annie. They walked a few meters away and then Mark queried, 'Annie, I guess Peter was after that camera. What's in there?'

She looked stunned and confused, stammered and said, 'Umm… a couple of family videos. We watched them last weekend but I sincerely don't know why he would want to break into my room for it. I know he misses his dad but…I just don't know.'

He looked directly into her eyes, looking suspicious and said, 'Annie, you knew James was alive. Why did you let us do it?'

She stood there, absolutely dumbfounded and gazing into his eyes, she burst into tears. 'I never knew it. I swear! I never knew he was ….' Mark shushed her in the middle of her statement.

'Let's talk about this at home' He said.

Beginning to feel a bit suspicious about how quick he was to silence her, she asked Mark while returning to Peter's ward, 'Did you know about this?'

'Let's talk about this at home' He replied bluntly.

At 6pm in the evening, the doctor assured Annie of Peter's recovery; that he was responding much better to treatment and could regain consciousness in the coming day.

Annie had not eaten anything since breakfast and though she wasn't concerned about food, Jane had to eat supper and Annie herself needed to take a bath. Although feeling reluctant initially to leave Peter for the house, Mark convinced her that it would be more prudent if she got some rest before the next day when Peter was expected to regain consciousness. They set off for the house and bought some food for supper.

At 9pm, having laid Jane to bed, Annie joined Mark at the hall. They knew they had a lot to talk about. She drew closer to him and asked, 'Where is the camera? Have you watched our videos?'

'I just can't believe you really made us do this though you knew James was alive', Mark said with disdain.

'I only came across this a week ago and I'm feeling much worse than you are. Please, stop accusing me. You are making me feel worse than I have been.'

'And you didn't delete it like he said you should? I can't believe he had acted so carelessly in recording that video' Mark burst out.

Surprised at his choice of words, she asked in a subtle tone, 'Mark, did you know something about this whole thing? Please don't lie to me.'

Mark denied knowing any more than what was captured in the video but Annie disbelieved that – He had blown his cover by his reactions and quickness to cut her in her speech back in the hospital. As he kept refusing to let a single word out, Annie walked out on him with tears in her eyes, refusing to be comforted. Mark, seated in the couch, was left in a complete dilemma – He knew the issue at hand was much complicated than Annie thought, and he had no idea where to start from.

He could end up letting out some very sensitive issues that could break her heart. Mark had gotten himself emotionally attached to Annie, and he knew James was the only reason he hadn't expressed his feelings for her. Annie had relocated to the guests' bedroom, the room Mark uses, since her bedroom's window was broken. Mark sat at the hall, feeling very uneasy because he could hear Annie's sobs from the room and he couldn't bare it. He had to find a way to console her.

Some moments later, he went after her. She was seated on the bed, sobbing pitifully. He apologized to her, told her that James had to fake his death because he had gotten himself in a mess which could risk the lives of not only him but the kids and hers as well. For the details, he assured her he would tell her the next day.

She persistently asked him to tell her where she could find him but he insisted he had no idea. She slept and with Mark lying beside her, she recalled living through those sorrowful days with Mark – her only and constant comforter.

Annie just couldn't bear to believe that it was all a drama. Mark took her in his arms and cuddled her but Annie, in order to quickly get the sorrow out of her head, got up, stripped herself stark naked and lured Mark to make love to her again.

CHAPTER 4

Annie was up by 5am to do the daily chores. An hour later, Jane joined up with her in the kitchen to help prepare breakfast. Some minutes later, they were done with breakfast and just when Mark was joining them at the table, Annie's phone rang.

She answered the call which lasted less than half a minute. She cut the call and racing towards her room, she exclaimed exuberantly, 'Good news! It's good news! Finish up your meals quickly and let's leave.

Peter has recovered.' Mark and Jane were equally excited and jubilant. They raced off to freshen up, ignoring the meal. In about fifteen minutes, Annie was ready with Peter's breakfast all setup and in a basket. The others joined her in the car and they drove off to the hospital.

While in the car, Mark reminded Annie that Peter had seen the video but they had to make sure he told no one because if the news reached the wrong ears, they would be as good as dead. She nodded in consent to him but she was actually only thinking of Peter the whole time.

Jane, overtaken by curiosity began to pester them with questions, incessantly probing them on what Peter had seen in the camera. However, they felt they couldn't trust the little kid with such classified info. Annie talked her down and promised to tell her everything once they get Peter out of the hospital.

They arrived at the hospital and made their way towards Peter's ward. They met the doctor in Peter's ward and he assured them that Peter was doing perfectly well. However, he also told them he had called the police detectives and that they could be in anytime soon. Mark was very uncomfortable upon hearing that but Annie, knowing virtually nothing, had very little idea what the implications could be.

Annie and Jane hugged him with tears their eyes, telling him how much they were worried but Peter was ambivalent. Mark tried explaining to him that he couldn't tell anyone what he saw but he just wouldn't listen, neither did he utter a word. He was very mad at his mom for lying to him. Nonetheless, it was imperative that they reached a conclusion before the police arrived.

After much frantic efforts from Annie to convince him to accept their terms, Mark took charge of proceedings. He said to him, 'You are no longer a kid and you understood exactly what your dad said in the video. If any other persons got to find out about this, you, your mom, and sister would be as good as dead. Not even the police can be trusted – your father didn't trust them on this. Tell the police you wanted to buy a video game but your mom refused you money and that's why you did what you did – to get some money for it.'

The adults had made their point but resolute Peter didn't look like he wanted replace his legitimate reasons with a lie. The police came in about ten minutes and they engaged Annie first.

She told them that Peter hadn't said anything to her yet but they could find out for themselves. Her nervousness sent suspicious signals to the detectives but they didn't take it any seriously.

The detectives asked to speak with Peter privately. As Annie and co were walking out, one of the police personnel called her back and asked, 'You seem panicky, is there any reason?' She shook her head and walked out.

The police engaged Peter for close to fifteen minutes while they waited outside the ward and they had absolutely no idea what was transpiring between them. They could only hope Peter would say anything but the truth. Seeing that Annie was visibly nervous, Mark drew closer and patted her to calm her nerves. When the detectives brought their probing sessions to an end, Annie and Mark hurried through the door to meet them.

'Is everything alright?' Annie enquired tremblingly.

'Yes,' they replied, 'except that we think he may be hiding something but all the same, some details can be very confidential and irrelevant to our investigations. Our aim is to find out if it was a criminal case or it was just the little boy's naïve actions. Judging from evidence at the scene and the information gathered from you and the kid so far, we think it's more of an in-house affair.

We wouldn't be making any criminal proceedings or investigations but in connection with what we gathered from the boy, you need to see us at the police station for the furtherance of proceedings. Drop by the department later in the day.'

'Okay, but is everything alright?' She enquired worriedly. They assured her there was nothing to worry about but that it was a necessary part of their procedure.

Annie and the rest hurried to Peter as the detectives walked out and questions came swamping in from all angles – They all were desperate to hear from him what had transpired between him and the police. Much to their frustration, Peter still declined to tell them anything. Fifteen minutes passed and finding out nothing they said could make him cooperate, Mark was extremely pissed and asked them to walk out so he could have a private audience with him.

'What do you think you are doing? Being a tough guy? You are only acting dumbly and putting your family's life at risk. You know, your foolish deeds have caused your mom much trauma, and she attempted a suicide last night. I had to talk her out of it.

Now, I guess you want to help her die faster. Ask yourself – Who will cater for you and who would love you better than your mom has when she's no more? Don't think I will, because I'd be busy blaming you, and so will Jane. You are being two things; selfish and stupid. Wake up to reality and stop this nonsense. Be smarter – everyone wishes to find your dad but not everyone wants him alive.'

He walked out right after making his point and the others also rushed in. Mark and Peter had been close buddies but Mark had never been this mad at him. Those words cut deeply into Peter's heart. Annie walked in and sat by Peter on the bed and without saying a word, she cuddled him affectionately.

He burst into tears right away and confessed apologetically that he had told the police the very same words they had asked him to say to them. The news gladdened her heart and a comforting smile found its way onto Annie's lips. Jane joined in the hug and Mark, upon returning, did same.

Later in the day, doctor informed them Peter would be due for discharge the next morning. At 2pm, the carpentry service they had contacted called that they were at their address.

They left for the house right away, leaving Jane with Peter at the hospital. They got home and granted the carpenters access to the room so they could commence work.

While they did, Mark sat Annie down on the bed in the guests' room and said, 'Annie, we'll talk about everything pretty soon but now, just ensure your mouth is sealed about James; no matter what may come up. Like I said, even the police can't be trusted. Don't give them the slightest gist that James could be alive somewhere. It's very necessary and I'll tell you more stuff later.' Annie agreed. At 4pm, after the carpenters' job was done, they set off to the Police Department.

At the police station, Mark was asked to sit at the visitors' lounge while Annie was taken into a room for interrogation. The probing went on smoothly but just when everything was over and she was about stepping out, Detective Bridge enthused, 'What happened – has it got anything to do with your husband's death?'

'Pardon me!' said Annie, turning around abruptly.

'Never mind', Detective Bridge replied wryly.

Annie was confused and stood gazing at him curiously until Mark called her over.

'What did they ask you?' Mark enquired as they made their way towards the car. She told him the police had instructed that since the case was more of a disgruntled little boy's reactions, she had been ordered to take her boy to a clinical psychologist and a counselor every weekend for the next eight weeks. Though it wasn't pleasant, it was a much better directive than anticipated.

When they returned to the hospital around 6pm, they saw Jane lying on the hospital bed, coiled into Peter's arms. They sat on the couch with Annie's head comfortably resting on Mark's shoulders and in a few minutes, they too fell asleep.

CHAPTER 5

Peter was discharged around 11am the next day. They passed by a restaurant and arriving home at 1pm, they requested that Mark told them what was going on but he insisted he would tell them the next day.

At 9pm in the evening, when the kids were asleep, Annie made her way into the guestroom to get her much needed answers. Without knocking, she ushered herself into the bedroom.

Mark had just finished bathing and was sitting bare-chested on the bed in a tiny boxer shorts. He smiled at her but she was in no mood for smiles.

She sat beside him and said, 'Hey Mark, I'm here now and I need no more excuses. I want to know all there is to know'.

His smile fainted and he stammered, not knowing where to start from.

'Annie, I'd... I'd always not wanted to be the one to tell this story but now it's impossible not to. I need you to know that I wasn't privy to James' actions and had never wanted James to do whatever stuff he did.'

Annie placed her palms into his and said, 'Mark, you should understand my desperation to know the truth. You were involved one way or the other and you can make things right by starting to tell me. I know it's gonna hurt but I've psyched myself up for this. Please, let's not drag this any further.'

Mark, still not wanting to speak out conjured some very obvious lies. She tried as much as she could to get the truth out of him but as this ineptitude of his continued, Annie could take it no more.

She blasted out at him rudely, ran into her room and, being completely distraught, she cried bitterly. Annie was such a lady and had never been that rude towards him. Half an hour passed and when Mark realized he couldn't harness the feeling of guilt any longer, he decided to let the cat out of the bag.

He entered her room and found her awake. She was sitting on the floor with her back leaning on the bed and was visibly distraught. After Mark lowered his body to sit by her, she queried in a hysterical tone, 'What kind of a man fakes his death and leaves his wife and kids for over two years; and what kind of a friend partners such wicked deeds? More frustratingly, though their mischievous ways are obvious, they still seek to cover their trails.'

Annie was very hurt and felt betrayed, not just because of her husband but because she felt the man for whom she'd developed a strong amorous feeling for was involved in the beginning, never told her, and is still hiding the truth from her. As she kept on making more heartbreaking statements, Mark felt compelled to tell her everything; just so she wouldn't be bitter against him. He narrated:

"You know James and I used to frequent the Winstons Beach Club. One Friday night, while having some drinks with an extra empty chair to our table, we noticed a lady on one of the nearby tables. We stole glimpses at her and gossiped about her; wondering whether she came alone or was waiting for someone. Occasionally, a few guys would come sit by her but none lasted up to two minutes.

When she finally caught us spying on her, James quickly offered a wave and smiled at her. Some minutes later, when we were not looking, she came to us and asked if she could have a seat by us. We were already in an ecstatic mood so we accepted."

"She introduced herself as Vera and said it was her first time ever at a club. We introduced ourselves too, chatted and drank together. Although she was a teetotaler, she didn't say because she felt a little shy and thought it would be embarrassing. By the time we thought we should be leaving, she was totally drunk but we couldn't just leave her there in that state. We took her and upon reaching the base, James asked that I take her in to my suite since mine was more convenient. "The next morning, she had a hangover and she accused me of getting her drunk to sleep with her. I went through a hell of a time, trying to explain to her that I did nothing. At 11am, James came around. While I tried my hands on something at the kitchen, they were getting along with each other really well. I joined them later with the meal for lunch. She disclosed that the previous night was her first time taking in alcohol and that she came to the club because she was pissed at her dad and wanted a place that could calm her mood. I mentioned how she gave me a hell of a time trying to explain I didn't touch her sexually and she laughed it off hilariously. She whispered to my ears that she was a virgin and that she would have known if I touched her. Virgin or not, that wasn't my concern. Right after lunch, she said she had to go. We drove her to see James' place and then we took her to the club's parking lounge and she got into her sleek Bentley Bugatti – We could tell she was fabulously rich."

"We never heard from her until after a week, on a Sunday. She came to my place at 11:15am but since I was on duty at 12pm, she went over to James' place. Later in the evening, I met up with James and asked him what transpired between them. He said they only chatted, that she was just a lonely young lady who needed some attention and entertainment, that nothing silly happened.

Months passed by and though I was still in touch with her, she'd grown fonder of James since unlike me, he was very exciting. James and Vera became too close for my liking and I began to suspect there were stuff going on between them that I didn't know of. Anytime I confronted James on the issue, he brushed it off and said there was nothing more to it than I already knew of.

I did ask Vera a couple of times about them, but she always joked it off and said that I was jealous. Four months later, I was selected as part of the troops to be sent on peacekeeping at Syria and I had to be there for six months."

"A week after I had returned from Syria, Vera came to visit us and she was so excited to tell James she was three weeks pregnant. I was absolutely stunned because no one had told me a thing and I was highly disappointed and angry because I felt James had betrayed you. She even kissed him right before my eyes.

James signaled me to keep my mouth shut, that he would do the explanations after she was gone. More complicated was the fact that she said her dad whom we had never met and knew very little about wanted to see us. I was so angry that I couldn't wait for her to leave. I set off to my place, leaving both of them alone."

"The next morning, a postman delivered a letter from James. It explained how they both got themselves drunk one night, while I was in Syria, and when they failed to control their sexual urges, he ended up breaking her virginity. She was very disappointed and hurt the next morning and in order to console her, he asked her out and since then, they'd been intimate. He explained that I couldn't say a word to you nor Vera."

"I met up with him later in the day and it was then that he disclosed to me that Vera was the daughter of the most notorious drug baron in California – Max Manuel. He had never been and still has never been implicated due to his strong links with various high government officials who usually contract him to do their dirty work.

He robs, destroys and kills at will and no one dares to cross this guy's path. Against her father's wishes, Vera had always been a cool everyday-girl and took no part in his business.

He told me how Vera's former boyfriend was murdered by Max Manuel's gang after he had cheated and broken Vera's heart. We knew the man would be absolutely pissed that James had broken her virginity and yet deceived her, knowing he was married and with kids.

We knew he would definitely murder James and probably annihilate the rest of you if he found out."

"While James sought an alternative solution to this, we avoided meeting her dad for as long as possible. Someway somehow, information got to Vera and her dad that James was married with kids and Max began an underground dig up on James.

James convinced Vera that the rumors weren't true, that he was once married but got divorced along the way. Though she was partially convinced, it appeared her dad's thugs had found enough information and he required that James met him.

Obviously, telling him the truth was not an option, neither did we have a choice. Besides, Vera had threatened to take her own life if any of those rumors were true."

"With a one-week ultimatum fast running out and after careful deliberations, we came to an agreement that he had to fake his death, falsify his identity and smuggle himself out of the country – losing all contacts and relationships – in order to start a whole new life.

Then, you would join him after some months. It was just us and Teddy Pearl – a secret friend of his I never met – who knew about this arrangement. Teddy Pearl was just a bait name and since he always contacted us through public payphones, I never had his contact.

So as it were, I only knew my side of the plan, and the rest of the details were between him and Teddy Pearl. I just had to do my part of it and trust that they were going to playout their roles perfectly well."

"With just a few days to the end of the ultimatum, while I was with James at his lounge and discussing these matters, the never identified militant group launched their devastating airstrike attack on our base. War planes flew over the base, gunshots fired here and there and bullets flew all around. We had to rush out to a place of safety.

James explained that this was a perfect opportunity for him to disappear. Orders were thrown in here and there and the engines of the warships were ignited for battle against enemies en route the sea. Dead bodies laid all around the base and most of our planes were bombed before they could even fly. We made our way into the waters which were rippling with bullets all round and moving further into it was like approaching the cave of death itself. Suddenly, there was a deafening blast to a nearby boat which injured me as well."

"I found myself a piece of wood to hold on to and saw James swimming farther and farther away but then I passed out, only to find myself at the hospital. As you know, his body was not found in the waters and after spending three weeks at the hospital, I never heard from James.

There was no way of reaching the secret agent either since he never gave me his number.

I only hope that he didn't die and still believe he's somewhere out there."

Annie was devastated by this revelation. She picked herself off the ground, tears in her eyes, walked him out and locked her door. She wept bitterly throughout the night.

CHAPTER 6

5am the next morning, having endured a bad night, Annie walked into Mark's room and met him asleep in boxer shorts and a singlet. She sat beside him on the bed and rolled the sheets. Mark woke up and was startled to see her. She was wrapped in a white towel and it was obvious she had just come out of the shower. He tried getting himself up but she pushed him back onto the bed. She loosened her towel and got completely naked but he looked a little glum, unsure what her motives were.

'Annie, I'm sorry for...' She shushed him and kissed him passionately. Tears drizzled down her cheeks.

'It doesn't matter anymore, it's you who never left me and it's him who was unfaithful. I really hope he's not dead but it's you I love now, not him.

She stuck her hands into his boxer shorts and pulled on his dick; it hardened even more. Mark was absolutely speechless. He grabbed her breasts, groped and sucked them. She moaned. He turned her over unto the bed, spread her legs wide open, and caressed her clits. She moaned even more and was extremely wet. She pulled his boxer shorts down and guided his dick into her for a passionate round of sex.

Peter woke up and while he was going to fetch a glass of water from the kitchen, he saw Mark's door laying ajar and could hear funny sounds emanating from within. He peeped; his mom was bent over in the doggy style and Mark, sweating all over, was pounding her so heavily that she couldn't stop screaming. Peter banged the door shut and walked away, absolutely disgusted and pissed. They heard it and knew one of the kids had seen them but they were not gonna spoil the moment. She just managed to keep her moans undertone while they continued making love passionately.

Later in the day, Mark took them out to the beach to spend some quality time. Annie confessed to him that after all that James had done before his disappearance, she had absolutely no place in her heart for him. She thanked Mark for all the support and care and reiterated the fact that she had grown fond of him. Mark didn't hide his own longstanding affection for her either. They shared numerous hugs and kisses until Jane and Peter, returning with some kebab, caught them kissing passionately.

They spent three happy hours there before returning home. Although not absolutely furious, Peter raised concerns about why he saw them kissing when apparently, it was suggestive that his dad could be alive.

Mark apologized to him but he demanded more explanation from him for fucking his mother behind his father's back. Mark tried appeasing him with nice words but since Peter wouldn't step down, Annie felt frustrated and told him the story behind his dad's disappearance. After hearing that, Jane and Peter felt very disappointed in their dad but.

However, they understood perfectly that they could mention it to no one. Around 7pm, Jane walked to Mark who was alone in his room and told him he had her permission to marry her mom if he wished to. He was so happy and conversed with her till 9pm when her mom came to fetch her to go to bed.

At 10pm, Mark walked into Annie's room while she was in the bathroom and sat on her bed. She returned from the bath, singing passionately and completely naked. Startled to see him on the bed, she rushed back to the bathroom and wrapped herself in a towel before returning. Mark laughed hysterically.

'Why did you rush back to put this towel on?' He asked as she sat on the bed.

'I was shy. I didn't know you were here.'

'Really? what is there to be shy of? I've already seen everything.'

'Come on, don't be naughty.'

He laid her on her back, and unwrapped her from the towel. He smiled and stared her in the eyes but she looked away shyly.

'Come on, after all we've done? You can't be shy.'

'Oh Mark, umm… just quit the talking and do me.'

He pulled his dick out and when he was about penetrating her, she stopped him.

'Can I ask you something?' she said.

'Sure, anything.'

'You know your dick is so huge? It's much huger than his.'

'Oh… sorry. Does it hurt?'

'No… come on, I really love it. Makes me feel heavenly.'

'So…? May I?'

'Yea… just take it easy on me.'

'Alright, then you come fuck me.' He said, lying backwards on the bed.

She stood herself up, placed her legs at either side of his hips and squatted. She was already so wet that her vagina juice was dripping. She sat on his dick slowly and began to ride like a first-timer. He held her waist and pressed downwards so his dick got in deeper. She lost herself completely and he guided her to fuck really well.

I definitely would have cheated on James often if Mark had ever fucked me, she thought.

At about 1:30am, while they were asleep, they heard the kids scream. Mark, in his boxer shorts, sprang to his feet and raced for the door to go check it out while Annie, who was just in her panty, grabbed her nightgown to put on. As she started making steps towards the door, she met Mark walking backwards into the bedroom with a gun stuck in his face. Two other guys walked in and with one sticking a gun in his face, the other tied her hands behind her back.

She asked that they at least made her change into something more appropriate since her bare breasts and panty were exposed but they refused. They ceased all four of them and with their hands, legs and mouths tied, they covered their eyes with a blindfold, walked them into a van and drove them away.

After about an hour, the vehicle stopped and with their blindfolds still on, they walked them into some place. They sat them on the floor and removed the blindfolds. It was then that Mark noticed where they had been taken to.

CHAPTER 7

They were in a room surrounded by over twelve armed men. A door opened and Max Mayor walked in, taking a seat before them.

'Mr. I hear you are Mark, best friend of James, the alleged dead man. Am I right?'

'Yes, you are' replied Mark.

'Is your friend truly dead as we are made to believe?'

'He died during the attack on the naval base two years ago.'

'How sure are you and why do you think I should believe that?'

'I don't know why you won't want to believe that. It's a fate we all have to accept it.'

'Ha…ha…ha, that's funny enough. His corpse was never found. Besides, I have intelligence that this lady, her son and you have been acting strangely lately which we believe has something to do with your friend. I know he's not dead. Where is he?'

'If he's not dead, we don't know where he is because we've never heard anything from him.'

'Lies, these are lies' he said with a stern look, 'You are covering up for him at the expense of your innocent lives?'

He turned towards the kids and threatened them to speak but their mom stepped in.

'Please Mr.' she said, 'Please leave the kids out of this and let's talk this over. Please.'

'Okay lady' he said mockingly, 'Open your mouth and speak. I'm listening.'

She pleaded with him to let go every bitterness and pain but while she kept beating about the bush, he slapped Jane and she burst into tears instantly. Seeing firsthand how ruthless a man he was, Annie was compelled to move straight to the point.

'There was a recording... a video recording that James did. I never saw it until recently and when I declined to discuss the contents with the kids, my son was curious and anxious to know its contents. His actions led us to the hospital and the police.'

'You're making up a hilarious story. What proof do you have? Where is the video?'

Mark wouldn't have let a word out but for the sake of the kids and Annie who were pleading that he did whatever they asked.

'It's beneath the driver's seat of Annie's car' Mark said arrogantly.'

'You are sure of that? You won't like the consequences if you're deceiving me.' Max Manuel retorted.

'Yes, I know. I'm not telling lies.'

He ordered six of his thugs to escort Mark to retrieve the video camera. The kids were taken to a well-furnished but heavily guarded room at the very top floor of the huge mansion while Max Manuel had a private audience with Annie.

'Do you know your husband messed with my daughter's emotions and mocked my intelligence? Fuck him! Fuck the fuck that he fucked my daughter and not just that, he impregnated her.'

'Please... please... have mercy on us. At least for the kids' sakes. We knew nothing about his dealings with you nor your daughter. He always had reason to believe he was faithful. Trust me on this tape issue, I discovered it just a few days ago.'

'So where the fuck is your husband?'

'We don't know. We don't even know whether he is dead or alive.'

'Fuck you! I'll shoot you in the head if you don't speak up! Where the hell is he?' He threatened, pointing the gun to her head.

'Please... Please Mr., I swear we've never heard from him. We believed absolutely that he was dead till recently.' She said tearfully.

He walked out of the room, leaving her tied to a chair and under the watch of four strong guards. An hour and some minutes later, the other thugs returned with Mark and the video camera. They tied him to the seat next to Annie's and Max Manuel walked in some minutes later. He took the camera and asked Annie to show him the exact video but she couldn't locate it. Mark confessed that he had deleted the video right after Peter's incident. Max Manuel was extremely furious and smashed the camera to the ground. Annie pleaded and swore, telling her the details of the video but that didn't appease him.

Max Manuel left the room. Annie was untied and taken to the room where her kids were but Mark was left behind, still tied to the chair in just his boxer shorts.

7'oclock in the morning, Mark was released to join them and they were served breakfast but Annie was taken away to a suite equally as beautifully furnished as the other one, except that there were no guards in this one.

'Come sit and let's eat.'

She looked around and saw Max Manuel seated at a dining table to her left. She walked nervously towards him and took a seat.

'Enjoy the meal. Nothing to worry about.'

She sat down nervously, unable to touch anything. He served her plate with three slices of bread and poured her some coffee.

'Why are you acting so nicely to us this morning?' She asked worriedly.

'Well, you know… When someone is sentenced to the firing squad, they are asked to make their last wishes and even serve them the meal of their choice. So, if I'm gonna kill you guys, I should at least be nice to you. Nothing personal… strictly business.'

'How can this be business?' she said with tears in her eyes, 'You know we are innocent. You know, please.'

'Maybe… maybe you're innocent, but your husband – their dad – isn't.'

'Please don't kill us. Consider the kids, please.'

'What are you willing to offer as ransom?'

'I'll give anything… everything I have. I swear… I'll do anything to keep my kids alive. Please.' She said, sobbing pitifully.

'Just… Say no more words and eat. Perhaps, if I think I like you, I won't kill anyone.'

Without saying another word, she ate. One of the guards came in to clear the table. Max asked her to take a shower in the bathroom and make herself comfortable. He walked out and locked the door.

CHAPTER 8

Later in the afternoon, Max Manuel returned to the room. Annie was fast asleep on the bed in her nightie, her bare breasts exposed and her sexy beautiful thighs completely uncovered. He had a strong erection instantly. He sat on the bed and noticed she had no panty on. She had washed it and dried it in the bathroom. He stripped completely naked and lied down beside her. She tapped her on the shoulder and she woke up, totally frightened to see him by her. She covered her embarrassingly exposed nudity in the bedcovers.

He looked right into her eyes and said, 'You would do anything for your kids right?'

She nodded nervously with a bitter look on her face.

'I guess you know what to do then? You should do it really well.' He said, pulling the bedcovers of him and exposing his strongly erect curved dick.

Her heart began to beat irrepressibly and for over a minute, she couldn't touch him. He turned himself onto her, lifted her legs up and spread them embarrassingly open. She covered her vagina with both hands.

'You know this should be consensual right?' He said.

She nodded unhappily.

'Take them off then.'

Reluctantly, she slowly drifted her hands away and said, 'Please use a condom.'

He ignored her and pushed his dick unto her vagina lips but she wasn't wet at all. He caressed her clits with his dick to get her wet but all to no avail.

'Why are you crying? Look, I've noticed you are such a nice lady. I don't want to hurt you by penetrating your dry pussy. Ease yourself, okay.'

'Please, can't you stop this?' She pleaded tearfully.

'No, I'm sorry.'

He stuck his face between her legs and licked her vagina. She laid still, trying her best not to enjoy it. After a few seconds, she pushed his head out and shut her legs. He did it again and after a few seconds, she repeated it. He took two handcuffs from his drawer but she pleaded that she wouldn't repeat it. He licked her again and when she pushed him away once more, he cuffed her hands to the bed. He spread her legs again and licked her vagina zealously for so long. Her defenses were breached and she gave in to the sexual urges. He fisted her pussy till she experienced multiple squirting and body tweaking orgasms.

He stopped and asked, 'Should I penetrate you?'

'Please do.' She responded instantly.

He pushed his dick into her. It was so smooth and easy, warm and wet in there. She moaned pleasurably and he fucked her for hours. His aphrodisiac made him fuck for so long and when she felt she'd had enough and wished to stop him, she couldn't because of the cuffs.

He unlocked the cuffs and made her sit on him. She was so horny and sexually stimulated that she fucked as if there was no worry. It was the craziest fucking experience she had ever had. She felt completely sexually satisfied and lied happily beside him. Some minutes later – feeling completely guilty – she stood herself up, took a shower and asked that he let them go.

A guard led her to join up with Mark and the kids who had been taken to another part of the mansion – Vera's suite. The kids were having fun with a two-year-old toddler whiles Mark was chatting with Vera.

Immediately he saw Annie enter, he ran towards her and hugged her. He asked what happened with her but she said nothing bad happened, that he only asked her a lot of questions.

Vera introduced herself and she saw that truly, Vera looked so adorable and innocent-faced, unlike her dad. They shook hands and when she was told she was James' wife, Vera rendered a sincere and heartwarming apology to her, asking that she forgave her any inconvenience.

Vera told her how she got to find out from her personal secret agent that her dad had captured them. Apparently, she rang her dad early that morning, asking him to set them free and she cut short her trip to return that afternoon to ensure he did. Annie realized that was the reason he agreed to set them free, not because of the sex. She was so embittered but could tell no one her ordeal.

Meanwhile, Jane and Peter were so happy to see their baby stepsister and wanted to spend some time with her. However, they had to leave. Upon their request, Vera agreed to visit them the next day. When they got home, even after all that ordeal, everyone seemed fine but Annie was obviously not herself. She refused to share a room with Mark that night. The next day, Vera visited and they spent some nice moments together although Annie was in her bedroom for the most part of the period. Vera became a regular visitor for as long as the kids' vacation wasn't over.

After eight months, Annie was eight months pregnant and had become close friends with Vera but they never conversed about her dad nor James. She had also rejected Mark's proposal to marry her.

On one Saturday, Mark and Vera visited and they all went out to have some fun, together with the kids and the toddler. They returned home afterwards and while everyone was seated at the hall and relaxing, a heavily bearded man entered through the door without knocking. They rose to their feet and everyone found themselves a defensive weapon.

'Hello, please put your weapons down… It's me, James.' He took the artificial beard off. Truly, the face and voice showed it was him, only that he had grown overweight.

Peter and Jane ran happily to hug him. Annie burst into tears – feeling heartbroken, Mark was excitedly awestruck, and Vera was completely stunned and bitter. He himself had a heartache upon seeing Annie pregnant and Vera in his house. He bowed his head in shame as the kids accompanied him to a seat but the adults kept standing.

'Am I not welcome in my home?' He asked but none responded. 'Annie, you got pregnant? Really?'

Annie ran tearfully into the bedroom and Vera walked out with her child and drove off, leaving Mark and James alone with the kids. Mark also walked outside for some fresh air, leaving James alone with Peter and Jane. They asked him so many questions and expressed their grievances but in all, they were glad their dad wasn't dead.

Some hours later, Mark returned with Vera and they made their way to Annie's bedroom. James excused himself from the kids and joined the adults. He explained that he had been missing all that while because he was captured by the militant group and held captive until a serious inner insurgency led to their escape. Mark told him he was responsible for Annie's pregnancy and when that ensued in a brawl, Annie hit them with the most awkward news – it was Max Manuel's baby, not Mark's. They were hugely disappointed and disgusted and Mark was completely heartbroken but she refused to explain how it happened.

As they continued to express their disdain, she collapsed and was rushed to the hospital. Max Manuel rushed there too after being informed. Annie died in labor but the baby girl survived. Upon hearing the news, James shot Max Manuel dead on the spot, right in the hospital, and shot himself too to avoid a life sentence.

Vera became mother to all four kids and Mark, having no kids, acted as a father to them. Their parental duties led to an intimate relationship between them. Two years later, Mark resigned from the navy and got married to Vera.

I write under the pseudonym: Urquhart Randolph. I like to write great romance stories that take you on a blazing journey - tears, laughter (may be both) or just a steamy hot fun (perhaps all of them).

Please... leave a review, regardless if you think my book deserves 1* or 5 * let me know if you had enjoyed this great story?

THANK YOU ☺

WWW.GLOFTON.COM

Enroll in our VIP list.

Be the first to be notified on our latest published book.

Downloading for free gifts.